I0694204

BROKEN BLADE

AN
INFINITA SPIRES
SHORT STORY

BROKEN BLADE

CHRISTOPHER HOPPER

CONTENTS

INFINITA CODEX

For an even deeper experience, keep the Infinita Codex handy while you read. You'll find a vast glossary, organization histories, a character reference guide, timelines, and universe maps all at your fingertips. Proudly powered by World Anvil.

infinita.christopherhopper.com

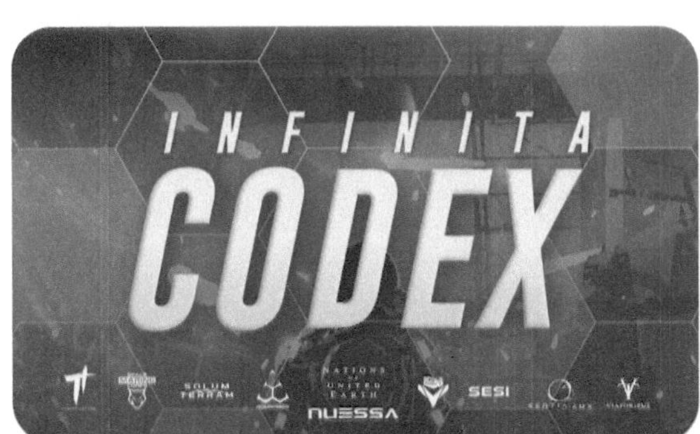

INFINITA
CODEX
SOLUM TERRAM
NATIONS of UNITED EARTH
NUESSA
SESI

PROUDLY POWERED BY

WORLDANVIL

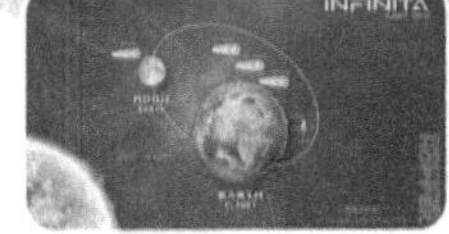

INFINITA

ASTRAEA STATION
INFINITA
NUESSA

AUTHOR'S NOTE

While this standalone story, available exclusively for you from my website, features a Solum Terram incog Tré Matthews. Since he's a pre-existing character in the main Infinita story, I recommend that you read or listen to book two, *Parallax Rising*, before diving into this thrilling installment of the Infinita Spies series. That way, you'll pick up all the subtle nuances and inferences that correlate with the main story and maximize your enjoyment. Thanks for reading and listening.

Christopher Hopper
Chaumont, New York
January, 2022

BROKEN BLADE

AN INFINITA SPIES SHORT STORY

"THEY'RE CIRCLING BACK," Marble said over team V-cog as the searchlights swept through the night sky. "Do not engage unless they spot you."

"Roger," came the general reply. It wasn't normal for non-officers to be giving orders, but this was his op tonight—his chance to impress Neon.

"How many?" Neon asked Marble as she pressed against his arm. They were holed up in Stuttgart's *rathaus*—an old city hall building. Every pane of glass in every perfectly square window had been broken a century before. Stuttgart, like all other cities this far south, had been abandoned during the Hundred Years Migration. But that didn't mean it was without treasure.

"Six," Marble replied.

"We can handle them, love."

"Yes. But all it takes is one to sound the alarm. And we don't know how many more might be in the surrounding area. We also have to assume they've sent at least one excipion."

A finger pressed into his shoulder. "I like you, Jonah. Tell me, are you this assertive in *everything*?"

"I… prefer my call sign, ma'am."

"And I prefer Jonah."

This was the first time he'd been alone with Neon. Unplanned. It's how the op had unfolded, at least that's what *Jonah "Marble" Finch* thought. *Tré Matthews*, on the other hand, knew that this op was as much about vetting Marble for promotion as it was securing buried treasure. Neon did nothing by mistake, and her singular presence by his side was part of her process. To try to unnerve him while simultaneously "inspecting the goods," as some said.

Matthews knew from watching Neon over the past few months that she liked the younger men, especially those who resisted her, at least a little. Too much, however, and she had them disappeared. He needed to play this right. Needed to secure his path toward eventually stealing the microdrive from her person. So he ignored her touch, for now, and avoided the glint in her dark eyes. Then he turned his attention back to the square out front. The recon pixie drones entered from the southeast along Market Street to his right.

"Two more coming up Hirschstrasse," Perish called out over V-cog.

"Roger. Everyone stay low," Marble replied.

"Why *Marble*?" Neon asked as the two new pixies appeared ten meters up, their lights eager to find quarry. "What's the story?"

"If I told you, I'd have to kill you."

"Is that so?"

"I can introduce you to the tombstones."

"My my, such a big game you talk."

"Games are for players."

"And you don't mean to play me, Jonah?"

He swallowed. Did she suspect him? He needed to stay focused. "I mean to get you out of here in one piece or die trying, ma'am." Too dramatic? Possibly. But he was, after all, trying to get promoted. *All syco-phants are welcome to apply.*

"Moving to the basement," Marble said over comms. "Ingress target building when clear." He turned to Neon and then motioned toward the stairwell in the back of the room. "This way."

"Lead on."

All that was left of Stuttgart was a dusty shell, barely tolerable in the winter nights and insufferable in the summer days. As April approached, the heat lingered longer after sundown, reducing available time for any excursions before heading back to the Tantum Terrae's headquarters twenty-four klicks northeast in Affalter-bach. By July, the city would only be home to the most resourceful creatures—humans not being one of them.

"How good do you think your intel is?" Neon asked as she followed him down the steps.

"It's solid."

"Enough to stake your life on it?"

Marble slowed.

"Let's venture a little wager, shall we, love? You lead me to gold, and I make you a Lieutenant. We all know that's what you want anyway."

"I want to make sure our cause stays funded."

"You want power, Jonah. Don't lie."

I figured it was best to ignore her statement. "And if the safe is empty?"

"I kill you."

He swallowed, cradled his rifle with his off hand, and offered to shake on it.

"You're that confident?" she asked.

"I would never risk your life for something I wasn't sure of, ma'am."

She laughed. "And you're a fool to think you'd ever have that kind of power."

His hand faltered.

But then she took it up. "Done."

The march down the old concrete steps continued until they entered a corridor that probably hadn't seen another human soul in a century—or so it appeared. The fact that any building still stood in this godforsaken country was a testament to Old German engineering. Where most nations built roads with twenty centimeters of base material, the Germans did it with forty. Where others spent one month on research and development, they spent six. And where any other local government leader might hide a safe behind a painting in their office, the mayors of Stuttgart had put one in the last place a would-be thief would think to look.

"How much further?" Neon asked from behind him.

"The sewer entrance is just ahead," he replied. "This way."

They carried on for another twenty-three meters before arriving at a rusted metal door with a broken placard that displayed half the word Sanitation. Sir Nigel Sallsworth's people had done a perfect job of covering Marble's tracks from the previous week. So far, there wasn't so much as a single scuff mark in the dust.

"You've been down here before," Neon said as Marble worked the door.

He paused, unsure if she meant that as a statement or a question. It was spoken to throw him off-balance. If he admitted to having been here already, then the bet he'd just made with her would be a false one, and she would kill him for it. But if he denied it, she might sense his duplicity.

"Yes. But only in V-cog." He tapped the side of his head with a finger. "Images and video from one of my sources."

"Mmmm."

The old hinges shrieked in protest as the door yielded to his shoves. Marble shined his torch into the next room and looked around at the large pipes that came and went from ceiling and walls to floor. Whatever stench there may have been a century before was gone now, replaced with the passive smell of rusted metal. Not even mildew could survive under the heat of the oven this sublevel became in summer.

"Where now?" she asked, speaking into his ear from behind. It sent a chill down his spine.

"There." He shined his light on a metal panel marked Sub Electrical. The box was up a flight of stairs and along a raised concrete balcony. "Watch your step."

Marble led Neon up the steps, then knelt in front of the door and made a small show of blowing the dust from the panel's seams. Subtle things, he knew, often did more to convince the mind of truth than obvious things. But too much subtlety and the brain flagged the action as disingenuous. It was a balancing act some thought he'd mastered, but he was not foolish enough to believe he actually had. Anyone who read their own headlines usually ended up dead in his line of work.

The panel came open with enough pressure and revealed a nest of wires.

"Dead end," Neon said.

The sound of her pistol sliding from its holster quickened Marble's heart rate.

"That's what it looks like, yes. But…" He forced his hands in and spread them apart to reveal a dull metallic green back wall with an old tumbler-style lock to one side and a lever to the other. Neon knelt beside him and then holstered her weapon.

"Lucky for you."

"No luck involved," he said but then thought better of the statement.

"Oh?"

"Research. And a keen eye."

"You think highly of yourself."

He shook his head once, knowing Neon disdained misplaced hubris. "I think highly of people who kept discreet records."

"But not discreet enough for you," she replied.

Marble also knew how Neon loathed false humility. "We each have our talents. And our… weaknesses."

The part about there being a secret lock box down here was true. This was a very old nineteenth-century Carl Ade safe built in Stuttgart. But it wasn't filled with gold bars, at least not before a week ago. The door had been open when he found it, the contents long gone. He assumed valuables of some sort had once been stored here, most likely retrieved by the city's last mayor before moving north. Who knew? But the Tantum's obsession with antiquity and its religious pursuit of bolstering the precarious but still advantageous precious metals side of the crypto economy meant few paladins would question the validity of what Marble was about to uncover. He only hoped that Neon would be as gullible.

"Where'd you get the combination?" Neon asked.

He'd thought about this at length. Part of him liked the old heist stories where criminals could listen to the locking mechanisms by pressing an ear against the door. But that practice, whether true or not, had died almost two centuries ago with the last of the purely mechanical locks. To think that he had somehow kept the art alive didn't pass his own sniff test, let alone hers. Though, he had to admit, there was probably some Tantum paladin in her crew that knew how. *All the more reason to stay clear of the idea*, he'd reasoned.

With his typical suave Janusian air, he smiled at her, produced a small notebook from his black leather jacket, and undid the elastic band. "The mayors were foolish enough to write it down."

"Notebook looks a little new, doesn't it?"

He gave a soft laugh. "Ma'am, I just took a note."

"On?"

"The chicken scratch under the mayor's desk."

"So you have been here."

"I never said I hadn't," he replied coolly. "You asked if I'd been *down* here before. And I haven't. But I did plenty of exploring in the floors above."

While part of him worried that this answer might betray him, another part recognized the coy smile of a minx creep across Neon's face. She appreciated subtlety as much as he did, it seemed.

"Bravo. Now let's see if it works."

"Yes, ma'am." Just as Marble reached for the lock, a gel propellant pistol cocked behind his head. He hesitated.

"Something the matter?"

"No, ma'am." Then his hand went to work, following the combination he'd programmed himself.

"Twenty fourrrr…" He spun and then slowed the dial. "Sixteen." He worked the opposite direction. "Fifty nine." When the last number was settled, he put a hand on the lever. "You ready?"

The pistol's barrel touched the back of his oiled hair. "Ready."

Marble opened the door, shined his light inside, and heard Neon gasp.

WHEN MARBLE ENTERED the war room in the old Mercedes AMG building in Affalterbach, he found all of Neon's top generals sitting around the boardroom table, and the lesser ranking personnel seated or standing along the walls. Neon was at the head of the table, bordered by her daughter Gemma off her right hand. The younger Birdwhistle spotted Marble as soon as he entered. Neon did likewise, and he wondered if they'd be talking about him. Neon gave him a barely noticeable smile, while Gemma scowled.

"Let's get started, shall we?" Neon said to the room. "But before we do, I'd like to welcome our newest Lieutenant, Mr. Jonah Finch, following his successful foray in Stuttgart."

The people clapped for him, a few even patting him on the shoulder.

"Marble, dear? Anything you'd care to say?"

He bowed his head in thanks and caught Gemma's death stare again. "Uh, I just would like to say… what an honor it is to be counted worthy of serving in an organization that's meant everything to me and my family growing up. Without you, without the Tantum…? I'd be lost. So this… this is a boyhood dream come true, right here." He looked at Neon. "Feed the rock."

"Feed the rock," the rest of the room said and then clapped for him again.

"Alright. Let's talk about Protavis Industries," she said and then handed things off to Gemma.

FOR THE NEXT TWO HOURS, Gemma, along with at least three different generals called to expound on intel, outlined a Tantum-led multi-faction plan to destroy the production facility of Protavis Industries located 640 klicks due north. Hamburg, like all coastal metroplexes, suffered from two centuries of rising sea levels that forced the inhabitants to abandon certain sections of the city in favor of others higher up. But since the city was farther inland, connected to the North Sea by the Elbe River, it managed to retain much of its historic beauty while its leadership tried to work with, not against, the effects of climate change. The result was a warm weather paradise destination for tech companies looking to cater to their high profile investors. As such, the city felt as though it were living up to its nickname given centuries before: *Tor zur Welt*, gateway to the world.

Protavis Industries had been one of the first companies to invest in Hamburg during the close of the last century. Most private enterprises collapsed or were bought out by bigger companies in the wake of the Hundred Years Migration. But Protavis's commitment to build quality electrical parts for both planet- and space-bound enterprises meant it could feed from two troughs where many companies committed themselves only to one. "Double dipping" was the term its critics employed, but "success" was the word its investors used.

"We're going after its pride and joy," Gemma said during her briefing. A holo display lit up a specific section of the company's sprawling multi-hectare facility along the Elbe. "The Power Conditioner Manufacturing Plant."

The Protavis EM-1 PCU was the most widely used power conditioner unit in the system, installed on every legacy hab and dome settlement from Earth to Ganymede. Double-dipping lobbyists in both Solum Terram and Viatoribus politicasts meant that Protavis won no matter who was in power—that was the true secret of coming out on top. But the company had grown stronger in the last several decades by underbidding their competitors and landing its now famous exclusive deals with NUESSA. However, that also made it a perfect target for the Tantum Terrae. Especially now.

"This goes beyond hindering normal supply chains," Gemma said. "As you all know, the joint NUESSA/SESI Infinita Gate program is well on its way to constructing the abomination that threatens the fate of our entire species. But our esteemed engineers" —she nodded to several people around—"have noted that *Parallax One*'s specifications call for at least three dozen new EM-1's, all of which are currently being manufactured in Hamburg."

"So that's why we're taking it out," Marble said. "Kill the factory, kill the gate." He knew speaking up was out of turn, knew he was the low man in the pecking order, but he wanted to see Gemma react. If his presence was causing a rift between her and her mother, he could exploit that. Destabilize them, and maybe even get Neon off her game.

Gemma glowered at Marble, her eyes a roiling sea of pent up anger. But she refrained from acknowledging his outburst with anything more than her glare and went back to addressing the room.

The plan was straightforward and required four Tantum squads to infil over a minimally staffed holiday weekend, plant charges, and exfil before detonating.

Knowing that all Protavis buildings were highly secure and that even the most careful covert team would need to make plenty of noise to gain entry, Gemma had somehow managed to work deals with rival factions to create distractions throughout the city. While this wouldn't affect Protavis security's response to the break-in, it would keep city law enforcement occupied, and probably even distract the city's military.

"Who is it?" one Tantum higher-up asked.

"Members of Leonidas X will be creating distractions in the west, while Radio Ultra and a platoon on loan from the Bemba Militia will be working in the south and east."

"Do we really need them?" the first man asked.

"I second the question," said another general. "Leo X thinks we're sellouts, the Bemba think we're weak, and the dreadlocks are tweaked out of their minds."

"And yet none of them are a match for us, now are they, gentlemen," Gemma said. "If you have some reason beyond not liking them, by all means, speak up. But as far as I'm concerned, they're getting paid to be cannon fodder. Unless you'd like to take their places?" She let the question hang in the air just long enough for the room to feel uncomfortable. "Wonderful. General Klipsch? It's all yours."

The flight north was uneventful, at least as far as enemy detection went. Well, Marble supposed that depended on which enemy he was worried about: those discovering the Tantum's movements or Gemma fileting Marble's soul with her eyes. She sat across from him in the shuttle, never once looking away. Marble, on the other hand, used the flight to sleep and settled his base-ball cap over his eyes. He'd occasionally look up as he adjusted himself in the chair, and still, Gemma was watching. He tried winking at her once, but the action elicited nothing. Not even a sneer. The woman was as cold as ice.

They landed in *Flughafen Hamburg*, Hamburg Airport, in the Fuhlsbüttel quarter of the north district. All V-rec and shuttle ident codes were accepted by tower control, and within ten minutes of landing, all four TT squads were in unmarked hover trucks heading west for Protavis. Marble watched as fireworks sailed over the skyline and blossomed into reds, greens, blues, and yellows. He imagined hearing crowds cheering beneath the explosions. Smelled the salted street foods roasting on spits. Heard the live bands lining the closed off street. He'd been to so many festivals, so many celebrations. But none of them to enjoy, at least in the ways that civilians did.

Eventually, the vehicles pulled into a nondescript parking lot bordered by tall palms. It had minimal overhead lights and was far enough from the highway and buildings that no one would inspect let alone notice a half dozen blacked out hover trucks sleeping through the midnight hour. The teams assembled at the rear of each vehicle, secured their weapons, ordnance, and black body armor, and then ran comms checks with their team leads. Marble carried a Hermann & Gruber HGRD-40 full-auto .40 caliber gel-propellent assault rifle with four thirty-round magazines and a Vicker 15-GP 9mm gel-propellent pistol with two ten-round magazines. He also packed two CTS Tactical flash-bang grenades and a Ka-Bar combat knife. As for larger munitions, the teams each carried materials enough for six

Uranitex uranium-laced nano-composite plastic explosives—enough to level each objective and then some. If the Tantum did this right, Protavis Industries would never recover this site. Granted, Sallsworth had already pulled his shares from the company's holdings weeks ago, much to the chagrin of the board, so he wouldn't be affected. But the secretary general promised not to be gone forever. Protavis would retool one of its many locations to make power conditioners again, and Sallsworth would reinvest at the bottom, standing to make more meteoric gains. But that move would be years from now, and *Parallax One* would have to wait just as long.

Gemma oversaw the op from the lead truck and, in a surprise move, Neon decided to replace the team leader for Squad Four—Marble's unit. The mother and daughter had a short-lived argument that made everyone in the taskforce keep their distance. In the end, however, there would be only one winner.

"Let's move out," Neon said and then ordered Perish to lead Squad Four under the highway and toward Protavis Industries's south fence, while Teams One through Three split up to their respective approach vectors.

V-cog integrated night vision goggles made moving through the shadows easy. Fortunately, Marble had plenty of experience with them—or rather, Matthews did. Marble might need to make a few mistakes here and there, especially if it allowed Neon an opportunity to school him.

"Shit," he said, pausing to fumble with his NVG's. "I can't get the—"

"Focus?" she said, coming up beside him. "Here. Let me take a look, love." A beat later, her moist breath graced his cheek as she adjusted the diopter for him. "Better?"

"Much. Thanks."

"Don't mention it." She didn't move. And for a split second, there was something akin to an electric charge that seemed to pass between them.

"Squad Four. What's the holdup?" Gemma's voice said over team comms.

"Issue with my NVG's," Marble said. "But I'm all set now."

"Keep moving."

"Roger."

Marble's unit arrived at the security fence and made short work of the chain links using a plasma cutter. Then they crossed the south lot, avoiding security cams marked on their topographic map overlaid in augmented reality via V-cog, and crept into the shadow of their target, the Power Conditioner Manufacturing Plant's South Quad designated Fabrication and Assembly Hall One. The other three targets included Research and Development Labs, the Quality Control Facility, and the Main Storage and Shipping Bays.

Squad Four's entry point was a basement window into a maintenance corridor. Only one camera surveilled the hall and could be easily overcome by nanojack tech—nanobot infiltration and signal hijacking. Two operators cut the glass, and the unit dropped in one at a time. Marble stayed in the shadows as a tech named Spitz rushed the surveillance camera. From a blind spot beneath the unit, Spitz placed a small device on the chassis and then cogged out while he directed the nanobots from inside V-cog. Three seconds later, he gave a thumbs-up. "Loop, good to go. Stand by for secondary effect."

The impressive thing about nanojack tech was that it not only overcame individual surveillance cameras and sensors, but if the operator was able to get through the needed firewalls, it could also compromise entire security networks through daisy-chaining. Granted, it wasn't foolproof and didn't work on every system, but Spitz had plenty of experience. After another few seconds, he finally said, "I have control."

"Perish," Neon called. "Lead the way."

And just like that, Squad Four had free rein in Fabrication and Assembly Hall One.

"TELL ME, LOVE," Neon said to Marble as they weaved in between fabrication equipment and headed toward a massive assembly line of sleeping robotic arms. The glossy white hardware with red text signifiers gleamed in the generic LED strip lighting along the floor. "Have you ever done something this significant before?"

"Demo work? Sure. Plenty of times."

"That's not what I asked."

He slowed to look at her. "You mean in terms of the effect it will have?"

She nodded once.

"No, I… I suppose not."

Neon pulled something from her kit, grabbed his wrist with one hand, and placed the object in his open palm with the other. "This"—she forced his fingers over a cube of Uranitex and squeezed—"will bring an industry to its knees. From right here, with this"—she shook his fist again—"you will make *Telemine* Station stop dead in its tracks. And with it, the abomination. It's never Goliath who wins. It's always the shepherd boy with the five smooth stones."

"Six, at least tonight."

She smiled at him and then pulled his fingers back. "Add your half."

"My half?"

"Of the compound?"

"Right. I'm… of course." He pulled his Uranitex cube from the small of his back and stuck it to hers. Then Neon added the blasting cap, battery, and remote detonation receiver. She brushed the tops of his fingers with her palm when they were done.

"Get used to having so much power in your hands, Jonah."

"Yes, ma'am."

"And please stop calling me that. To you, when we are alone like this? I'm only Magnolia."

"Uh… yes, ma'amm-Magnolia." He returned her smile. "Thank you."

"No, Jonah, love. Thank *you*."

She directed his hands to place the explosive on a support beam. It really didn't matter where this device went; the damage would be catastrophic. But the support was closest, and she seemed to enjoy making a show of their collaboration. On the nose? Completely. But it also meant she was letting her guard down with him, so he went along—the dashing young novice under the cougar's skilled hands. They pressed the bomb against the steel support, armed the device, and then called it in.

The blinking red LED flashed in Neon's eyes as she rested her cheek on the plastic explosive. The light caressed the shape of her face, neck, and collarbone. "Potential energy is in everything," she whispered. "You just need the right conditions to let it out."

Marble nodded. For the first time in Tré Matthews's career, he actually wondered if he would be able to survive the explosion to come.

WITH ALL TEAMS having reported in after ten minutes, it was time to exfil the target area and get clear of the Hamburg-Nord district. The cells of Leonidas X, Radio Ultra, and Bemba Militia soldiers were in position, waiting on Gemma to give the word, and the greatest fireworks display since the Migration Wars erupted over Germania. Neon asked Marble to help her down from a waist-high crosswalk while she zipped herself up when a flashlight appeared from a doorway to the west.

"Hey! Who are you?" a security guard said. "Hands where I can see them!"

"That's our cue, Jonah, love." Neon whipped her own Vicker 15-GP off her hip, leveled it with the guard in the distance, and fired. The *bang-bang-bang!* and bright light shocked Marble out of whatever hedonism he'd enjoyed at Neon's instruction. But so did his failure to find the microdrive rumored to be on her person. He would need to be more thorough.

The guard slumped in the doorway, but there were sounds of footfalls coming from the hall. Neon's gunshots had stirred the bee's nest. "Spitz?" she asked.

"I'm sorry. Looks like someone backdoored our backdoor. I'm locked out of the system."

"Then we're doing this the old-fashioned way. Moving to Hotel Niner," she said.

"What the hell was that?" Gemma asked over the squad channel.

"We're taking care of it."

"No. No you're not. I'm reading multiple units converging on your location, mother dearest."

"I said, we're handling it."

Gemma paused as if trying to temper her frustration. "Let me know when you're clear."

Perish wasn't two meters from the door leading to a side hallway when a security guard swung around the corner and fired a full-auto stream into Perish's chest. The sound came out as one long *brrrrrrah!* and shredded the TT's chest armor. The strobe light effect made the blood spray seem to float in slow motion while Perish flew backward and crashed on the floor.

Marble instinctively put an arm around Neon and pulled her behind an I-beam while the squad took out the security guard and two more behind him.

"Clear," Mouser announced and then cross-checked the hallway with Bevitz before entering.

"You okay?" Marble asked Neon.

"Oh, you're cute, love." She shoved his arm away and strode after the squad filing out the door.

"Perish's body?" Marble asked.

"Leave it."

Marble ground his teeth and reminded himself that these were not his people. Not his unit. "Roger."

He followed Neon into the hallway and double-checked the team's six. A single security guard entered the corridor some forty meters behind them. Without the aid of NVG's or knowing exactly what he was looking for, the guard wouldn't see the squad for another few seconds. Marble could take the shot now, and the man would never know. Or… maybe it was a situation he could use. Sometimes the ideas came to him in the moment, like improvising music. Only this was improvising death.

"Anything on our tail?" Bevitz asked from point position.

"Negative," Marble replied. "Keep moving."

Three seconds later, the security guard opened fire.

Marble yelled, "Contact rear," and threw himself on Neon just as several rounds bit into his back and shoulder. The armor stopped most of the bullets, but not all. Return fire came in a flash and cut down the guard.

"You're hit," Neon said to him and she rolled him over.

"And you're not," he replied between clenched teeth.

Neon started barking orders. "Frog, Sanchez, get him up and patch the holes. Florence, set optical charges. Everyone else, eyes up and watch our flanks."

Frog got Marble to his feet while Sanchez jammed the nozzle of a nanodermal spray can into a bullet hole in his shoulder.

"Son of bitch," Marble roared, but any further expletives were cut short when Sanchez pulled the trigger and filled the wound with the field med. Marble ground teeth and grunted until the burn subsided—that was until Sanchez plugged two more holes he found.

"We gotta keep up." Frog gestured to the squad now dropping out of sight down a stairwell. A military unit wouldn't have left them behind. They also would have carried out Perish's body. But this was far from Marble's military days. He was outside the wire in more ways than one.

"Can you still shoot?" Sanchez retrieved Marble's HGRD-40 from the floor and held it up.

"Hell, yeah." He fought the agony as he shouldered his weapon, but the painkillers were starting to kick in. "Let's do it."

More security forces fed into the hallway as Marble, Frog, and Sanchez raced to keep up with the team. They fired .40 caliber three-round bursts right, left, and rear as enemies stepped in to stop them. Marble, however, drilled each man and woman in the chest, center mass—one shot, one kill, never missing. He didn't even need tweak code for this, just years of raw military practice. But he'd need to blame his accuracy on tweaking if Frog or Sanchez lived long enough to ask questions. He couldn't afford to give someone like Gemma any more reasons to doubt his fabricated backstory.

By the time they reached the top of the steps, the hallway behind them was teeming with security. But all it took was for one guard not wearing an IDF chip coded to the team's freq to pass by Florence's optical charges before the hallway turned into an inferno. The explosion threw shrapnel at Marble, and he and his team members ducked as they took the stairs three at a time. The sound made Marble's ears ring more than they already were. But the boobytrap would buy them needed time.

The trio made it to the bottom step, doubled back behind the staircase, and descended into a sub-level service tunnel.

"Squad Four, ETA thirty seconds," Gemma said over V-cog. "Loading Bay Six, due east."

"Roger," Neon replied. "On our way."

Squad Four was together as they raced under the complex toward exfil. Just ahead, Marble caught sight of emergency lights, but they didn't belong to local emergency response teams; they belonged to the Tantum. While the squads were inside, the hover trucks got emergency lights and vinyl sticker sets designating them as NUE security vehicles. The disguises wouldn't pass close inspection, nor would the V-rec serial numbers find matches in the national database, but they didn't need to. They just needed to give any would-be observers no reason to doubt that Neon's forces were the good guys.

Marble jumped in the back of the first truck, ushered in by Neon herself. "You good?"

"Bruised but not broken," Marble replied.

"We can remedy that. Everyone else?"

"All squads clear of engagement zones," Gemma said.

"Good. Get us the hell out of here, love."

"Aye aye, mother dearest."

MARBLE HAD a perfect rear-facing view out the back window when the order was given to detonate the bombs. He'd seen his share of explosions in his day, responsible for half of them at least. But the Uranitex charges that took out Protavis Industries in Hamburg-Nord that night exceeded anything he'd ever witnessed.

The Uranitex alone would have been destructive enough. Stuff was demonic. But the simultaneous eruptions of the plastic explosive, the fusion energy equipment, and the battery storage devices, not to mention whatever other fuel and power storage units were on site, made for the single largest destructive force Marble had ever seen outside of an orbital magnetic rail cannon strike. He felt the heat through the armored glass as the fireballs billowed skyward. He sensed the tremor in the ground travel up through the repulsor chassis. Felt the truck lurch forward from the blast wave.

Strange, he thought, reflecting on how much death and destruction he'd been a part of. Today, he was employed by the Solum Terram, doing incog work against the Tantum Terrae. Tomorrow, he could be paid by the Viatoribus to undermine the Sentia Aux. He was an equal opportunity saboteur, and in this line of work, crypto was king. One needed to keep their options open, and Marble needed to get this job wrapped up.

Four Weeks Later

MAGNOLIA DIDN'T KNOW IT, but this was the last time she'd sleep with the man she knew as Jonah "Marble" Finch.

She traced the scars on his shoulder with her finger. "You've never told me, love."

"Told you what?"

"Marble. Where you got the name."

"Tough on the fist, but smooth to the touch."

Magnolia laughed and kissed his skin. "Adorable. And completely obnoxious."

"Hey. You asked."

"I did." Her face flattened. "And I want the real story, love."

Marble sighed and then pointed to a scar in the middle of his sternum. "I used to run with some kids who dropped out of boot camp. Thought they were too tough for the system. That they broke it when they went in and the sergeants had no choice but to kick 'em out. Bullshit, right? But that's how you reason things when you're young.

"So we're a few beers past our limit when these rich types walk into a bar we frequent and tell us to get lost 'cause they need the booth for important business with the owner. My guy Johnny recognizes one of the sleazy suits from the verb, a Viatoribus big shot, and realizes this is a meeting to discuss space dev. So Johnny tweaks out and goes full throttle at the guy. Adrenaline code times ten, right?"

Magnolia nods, her eyes filling with mounting interest.

"But these bastards are ready, at least their private security is. A few people get shot, others get some broken bones, but me? I get stabbed right the hell here." He points to his sternum. "It was a goddamn miracle. One centimeter to the left or right and I'd be dead. Craziest part is that the knife blade broke, if you can believe it. Personally, I think it was already a busted blade. Or maybe somebody saw it wrong… I never got a look." He wrapped an arm around Magnolia. "So they started calling me the Marble Miracle. And boy did it suck."

She chuckles again. "And why's that?"

"Because everybody and their brother wanted to sneak up behind me and take a shot at stabbing me in the chest to see if the legend was true. Was a pain in my ass."

"And your chest." Magnolia pretended to stab him in the heart, to which Marble faked a death scene but then pulled her into him and kissed her long and hard.

After another few seconds, she said, "I'm going to use it tonight for the first time."

Marble considered asking her to clarify, but the tone of her voice made him think better of it. This was it. A black swan. An unforced secret in exchange for all the things he'd done for her.

"I'm going to kill the secretary general in V-cog."

"Gaia's Blood? You're sure it's ready?"

"Of course." She pulled back and eyed him. "Why?"

"I just don't want you getting hurt."

"Mmmm. Maybe I need you to come along to take another bullet for me."

"Hey, it was at least three."

She kissed his scars again. "It certainly was."

"When, tonight?"

Neon ignored the question. "My daughter's on the way. You need to leave."

"You sure? 'Cause the three of us could—"

"You're leaving, broken blade boy."

He gave her a disappointed look but then smiled. "Until next time."

"Oh, indeed, love. And it won't be soon enough. Now leave before I have to kill you."

"Yes, ma'am." He stole one more kiss and then rolled off the bed naked.

MARBLE WASN'T HALFWAY down the hall from Neon's bedroom when Gemma came around the corner. "You screw her again?"

"Hi, Gemma. Good to see you too."

"Yeah. Only not." She stepped in front of him. "Listen. I know you and I aren't on the best terms."

"Really? 'Cause you're practically gonna be my stepdaughter by the time—"

"I know who you are, Marble."

This sent an adrenaline surge through his body. But he'd learned to master that impulse and refused to let his surprise show. Too many good opportunities were missed because people didn't know how to control their amygdala. "And who am I, Gemma?"

"You're an ass kisser who has no place in their organization other than to serve as cannon fodder."

"Ouch."

"And I don't trust you."

"Well, the feeling is mutual."

He tried to step around her, but quick as lightning, she grabbed his thumb and rolled his wrist over, and when she had control of his arm and got him on one knee, she jammed her thumb into a scar from bullet wounds.

"The hell is wrong with you?" he moaned, genuinely surprised by her speed. She had to be tweaking.

"I don't want you in my mother's life. And where she's too weak to see through your charade, I can guarantee you that I am not. Consider this your final offer to leave without a bullet in the back of your head. You will never speak of this, of us, and if the authorities come searching through Affalterbach, we'll come searching for you. Copy?"

"Let me go."

"*Copy?*"

"I copy."

"Good." She released him. He hit the floor hard.

Then Gemma stepped over his body and strutted toward her mother's quarters.

"Bitch," Marble said.

Gemma raised a middle finger behind her back. "You ain't seen nothing yet."

⁂

"Matthews," Sir Nigel Sallsworth said from inside a hosted V-cog lobby. It was a simple London café, and he sat at a window-side table sipping earl gray.

"I have them."

Sallsworth balked, but only for a second. "The activation key?"

"And the incog list." Matthews pulled a manilla envelope from inside his black leather jacket and slid it across the table. It was all for show within V-cog; a manila envelope could no more hold the necessary data than a teacup hold a pond. But the virtual transaction was legitimate, and Sallsworth watched the items populate his inventory. He would need his people at Lotus Labs to verify everything, of course, but it looked legitimate.

"What's your status?" Sallsworth asked.

"Burned. At least I will be. Gemma's on to me."

"That's alright. Your job is done. Get out of there and ping Victor. He'll send someone to pick you up."

"Roger."

After a moment, Sallsworth asked, "Tell me, how long before you think she notices that it's gone?"

"Uncertain. I replaced it with a fake. But I must warn you: she intends to come after you with the technology."

"When?"

"Soon. Could be tonight."

Sallsworth rubbed his hand on the manilla envelope. Lotus had already uploaded Gaia's Blood to his V-cog. Why not test the key himself? He smiled as he imagined the look of surprise on Neon's face.

"Will that be everything, sir?"

"Yes, Matthews. Thank you. Excellent work."

The spy nodded once, stood, and walked out of the café.

Sallsworth played with the envelope, spinning it lazily on the table. It seemed he had an announcement to make and a foe to slay. All in a day's work.

"WE'LL BE MONITORING," Gemma said as she walked behind her mother's desk and turned the chair for the Tantum Terrae's leader to sit.

"Good. Maybe you can learn a thing or two. Because when I'm done with Nigel, I'm going after the Master Sergeant and then Olivia."

The prospect of seeing Gaia's Blood in action delighted Gemma. Not to mention who else it would be used on after Nigel. The Marine known as Rook had slain her half-brother, Jack, and Olivia had clearly been seduced by the spacers. All of it was Evelyn Park's fault. The bitch. But Olivia had always been weak. Gemma never understood what her mother saw in the woman. Regardless, she had it coming. They all did.

Despite what Gemma knew was to be a night of assassinations unlike any other, something gnawed at her like a mosquito bite in the middle of the night. Jonah Finch. She didn't like him. Didn't trust him. But why? It was more than his infatuation with her mother, more than his obvious lust for power. *God, he was so annoying.* A sycophant to rival the rest. But was that all? Was there something else behind the quest to bed Neon and prove himself faithful? She suspected there was, but she had no proof. And her mother was blind to his ways. Distracted. And insufferably careless.

A spark flickered and flashed out in her memory like someone trying to start a fire with a flint.

"What is it, love?" Neon asked.

"Nothing. I just… I have something else I need to look into. Research, that's all. Happy hunting, mother. Always Earth."

"Always Earth forever."

GEMMA LEFT her mother's quarters and headed straight for the lab. Aside from monitoring her mother's assassination of the secretary general, Gemma needed access to the recon pixies. After making sure her team was squared away, she pulled up a V-cog control menu for a drone sleeping in Stuttgart. Within seconds, the small ariel recon device was airborne and headed across the city for the rathaus.

Instead of diving into the basement where the team had already been, Gemma pointed the pixie toward the spark of a memory.

"The mayors were foolish enough to write it down," Marble had said to her mother about the safe's combination; headquarters had monitored the entire conversation. "The chicken scratch under the mayor's desk."

And that's where Gemma was headed now. She flew the pixie up city hall's north face to the fourth level, through a blown out window, and down a hallway following the dusty placards to the mayor's office. Amongst the gutted furniture that spewed stuffing and springs like dead animals in a forest, Gemma spotted the carcass of the mayor's desk. A leg was missing, causing the boxy-looking object to pitch forward and to the right. She circled around, dropped under the desk, pointed the pixie's camera straight up, and began her search.

"MOTHER," Gemma yelled in Neon's ear.

Two lab techs were behind her—one, her friend Dr. Felicity Morrow. "Gemma, you know she can't hear you clearly. And the construct—"

"Is closed until termination! I know. But I have to try." She shook Neon's arm. "It's a trap, mother! He has it too."

"Gemma, please."

"No!" She threw Morrow's hands off her. "This was a setup."

"And you'll cause her to lose focus if you keep this up!" Morrow finally managed to overpower Gemma's grip and pull her away from Neon. "You have to stop touching her."

Gemma stood, panting. Hands balled into fists. Heart feeling utterly helpless as her mother marched into a trap. "It was *Finch*," she spat at last. "He stole her microdrive."

"With... with the key code?" Morrow asked.

"With everything." Gemma studied her mother's sleeping face. "I've never hated being right this much in my life."

"Come on," Morrow said, tugging on Gemma. "We can monitor the attack."

"She wants to duel with him."

"And she can take him."

But somehow, Gemma didn't share Morrow's faith. Sallsworth was a dangerous man who had sent a spy to play a dangerous game. She reached for her mother's forehead but held short of stroking it. Instead, she repeated the words she'd spoken earlier, only this time, she feared they were said in vain. "Happy hunting, mother. Happy hunting."

Gemma distanced herself from the other techs and took a seat in the lab. Only Morrow paid her any mind but knew better than to speak. A simple look of reassurance. A nod. And nothing more.

Gemma logged into the lab's V-cog observation suite—a design of her own making. She could have accessed this from her mother's room, but she needed the distance. Needed to let the huntress stalk her prey undistracted, just as Morrow had said. Still, not being by her mom's side ate away at Gemma.

I'm still here, mother, the young woman thought and then pulled up the suite viewer.

Neon fought Nigel back with a sword, forcing him into a billiard room off the kitchen. The man grabbed desperately at a ball and hurled it at her. He was acting. Toying with her.

Bile rose in Gemma's throat, but she willed her anger back down. "Come on. *End him.* Just do it now."

But the fight continued, mostly one sided, as Neon caught a second billiard ball and threw it back while rushing him with her sword. Nigel fell into a bookcase, and Neon stabbed him in the thigh.

"Just finish him," Gemma blurted out. She sensed the lab techs wince. But still her mother took her time, following her prey into a living room where Nigel took up a fire poker in addition to his sword. Gemma guessed her mother was the better master of arms, but in a competition where Nigel held a dark secret, the game was uneven—at least that's the way it felt.

A globe of Mars hit the floor and rolled from its base, and still the pair thrust and parried, Neon using her rapier, Nigel his sword and poker. At last, she stripped him of his sword while jabbing his arm and stomach. Neon spoke of her imagined trysts and travels with him, while Nigel continued to back away, hemorrhaging blood. But it was all for show. He even pushed through the French doors and pressed himself against the railing where she removed his left eye.

"My God," Gemma roared. "Kill him, mother!"

But still Neon continued on her self-righteous diatribe, pointing at his right eye…

Until a gunshot made Gemma leap from her chair.

A GRIEF-STRICKEN daughter burst from the lab and raced down the hallway to her mother's quarters, all the while watching the cat become the mouse and scurry for its life.

Neon had gone in prepared with her pistol. But seeing a new toy, she decided for a more dramatic slaying with one of the secretary general's mounted swords. If only she'd known Nigel was just as prepared with a gun of his own. Now, Gemma watched her mother's life signs in horror. Elevated heart rate, blood pressure, adrenaline—it was all there. Her brain believed what was happening, just like Gemma had designed it to. She had become the instrument of her mother's death.

As Neon looked at the blood streaming from her stomach, the revelation of the betrayal fell upon her. "*Jonah.*"

"Among his other aliases, yes," Nigel replied.

Gemma felt her heart sink. Surely, her mother must be remembering the warnings now.

Why not sooner? Gemma cried inwardly and cursed the fates.

The pair exchanged shots before Neon retreated up a flight of stairs. But her crimson trail betrayed her. Worse still, Nigel knew his home. So the secretary general diverted from the blood in the hallway, snuck up behind Neon through a bathroom, and aimed at her back.

"Mother, look out," Gemma screamed as she tore into the room where her mom reclined in the real. But she was too late—not that Neon could hear her anyway. Gemma's mother clawed at the curtains but refused to go down. That's when Neon screamed her daughter's name.

"I'm right here," Gemma replied as she sank to her knees and kissed the hand that had raised her. She knew every wrinkle. The curves of her knuckles. The shape of each fingernail. "I'm here."

But Gemma could not mourn. Not yet. Because it wasn't over. There was still a chance. So as Nigel forced Neon onto a balcony, the daughter summoned her rage and spoke it to the air.

"*Kill him*, mother. You can beat him."

Nigel raised his pistol to her face.

"It's not over! *KILL HIM, NOW.*"

"One round left, Nigel, dear," Neon said. "Use it wise—"

A muzzle flash.

A bullet hole.

And the back of Neon's head spewing open like a blood drenched rose.

Gemma roared as her mother's body jerked in the real. She looked up at a forehead with no fatal wound. Studied a face without anguish or fear. Just sleeping eyes and ruby red painted lips. Yet in V-cog her body tumbled over the ledge, fell through the air, and then landed on the pavement below.

A tremor shook Gemma, one that surged up from a dark tomb now left vacant. Soulless. With her mother's death came another ending. There, on the altar of that bloodied street, the one thing that made Gemma human was replaced by a burning rage that only wanted one thing to cure its malice.

Revenge.

INFINITA BOOK 3
KOGARASHI'S RUN

What will the explorers find at the second gate?

Will Secretary General Sallsworth destroy *Parallax One*?

And how will Gemma fill the power vacuum left by her mother's death?

Find out in book 3 of the Infinita series: *Kogarashi's Run*

Available in trade and mass market paperback, hardcover, audiobook, and ebook at **christopherhopper.com**.

Or your favorite retailers:

Amazon | Apple | Kobo

INFINITA BOOK 3
KOGARASHI'S RUN
CHRISTOPHER HOPPER
SECURE YOUR COPY NOW!

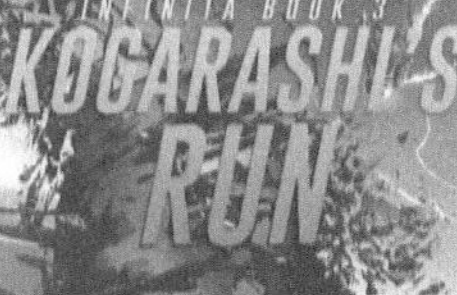
INFINITA BOOK 1
OBLIVION AWAITS
CHRISTOPHER HOPPER
INFINITA BOOK 2
PARALLAX RISING
CHRISTOPHER HOPPER
INFINITA BOOK 3
KOGARASHI'S RUN
CHRISTOPHER HOPPER

VIP

Become a VIP Club Member Today!

Membership is free, and you'll receive an official club poker chip, short story, and 10% off Christopher's store for life. Plus, you'll be signed up to get exclusive club perks in the mail and invited to join the private social media groups.

Visit christopherhopper.com to sign up now.

VIP
MEMBER
POKER CHIP

SHORT STORY

PLUS
EXCLUSIVE ACCESS TO
PRIVATE SOCIAL MEDIA GROUP

SCAN NOW

GEAR UP IN THE SHOP

Show your spacer spirit by purchasing the officially licensed Infinita t-shirts, hats, challenge coins, and more. From NUESSA and SESI to the Tantum Terrae and Sentia Aux, find your faction and chose your side at christopherhopper.com.

INFINITA
COLLECTION

FIND YOUR GEAR NOW!

ACKNOWLEDGMENTS

Once again, this short story would not be what it is without Matthew Titus, Jennifer Sell, Christie Strahler, Gary Guilmette, Tracey Beattie, and Neil Rubenking. Special thanks also goes to Dan Wong for his sharp attorney's eyes.

To my faithful alpha and beta readers for the thankless job of sweeping up the sawdust after the lights go out: Shane Marolf, David Seaman, Mauricio Longo, John Holley Jr., Kevin Zoll, Steve Janulin, John Walker, Jon Bliss, Mike McDonnell, Sean Ross, Eric Earley, Elijah Cole, George Hain, John Vermillion, Beverly Raymond, John Holley Jr, Brian Sinks, Joanne Sinks, Kathy Simonet, and Julia Camacho Monzon.

A heartfelt thanks goes to all the amazing spacers in my VIP club. Your encouragement and enthusiasm keep me positive and employed. I'm so grateful to have you as my most loyal fans.

Rebecca Woods and Daniel Wisniewski, thank you for bringing my characters to life for the audio version of this story. Once again, you have created a new piece of art from the rough medium of my words. Thank you for sharing your time and talents with us all.

I'm thankful for my fellow writing companions who know and share the highs and lows of publishing: Wayne Thomas Batson, Jeremy Davis, Jason Anspach, Jeff Chaney, Ken Lozito, Nicholas Smith, Gerry Riddle, Scott Moon, and Jonathan Yanez. Your friendship is a blessing.

Thanks to my daughter, Evangeline, for running my store and taking care of our customers, and to my son, Luik, for populating the Infinita Codex with all my world building content. You guys rock. Your dad couldn't do this without you.

And to my wife, Jenny. Thank you for charging through gates with me. I would be lost in the void without your hand to hold.

christopherhopper.com/infinitasecrets